THE IMPORTANT BOOK

The important thing
about a cricket is
that it is black.
It chirps,
it hops,
it jumps,
and sings all through
the summer night.
But the important thing
about a cricket is
that it is black.

The important thing about **GLASS** *is that you can see through it*

THE IMPORTANT BOOK

Words by
Margaret Wise Brown

Pictures by
Leonard Weisgard

HARPERCOLLINS*PUBLISHERS*

Manufactured in China.
ISBN 0-06-020720-5.—ISBN 0-06-020721-3 (lib. bdg.)—ISBN 0-06-443227-0 (pbk.)
Library of Congress Catalog Card Number 49-9133
For information address HarperCollins Children's Books
a division of HarperCollins Publishers
10 East 53rd Street, New York, NY 10022
12 13 SCP 20 19 18 17 16

The important thing
about a spoon is
that you eat with it.
It's like a little shovel,
You hold it in your hand,
You can put it in your mouth,
It isn't flat,
It's hollow,
And it spoons things up.
But the important thing
about a spoon is
that you eat with it.

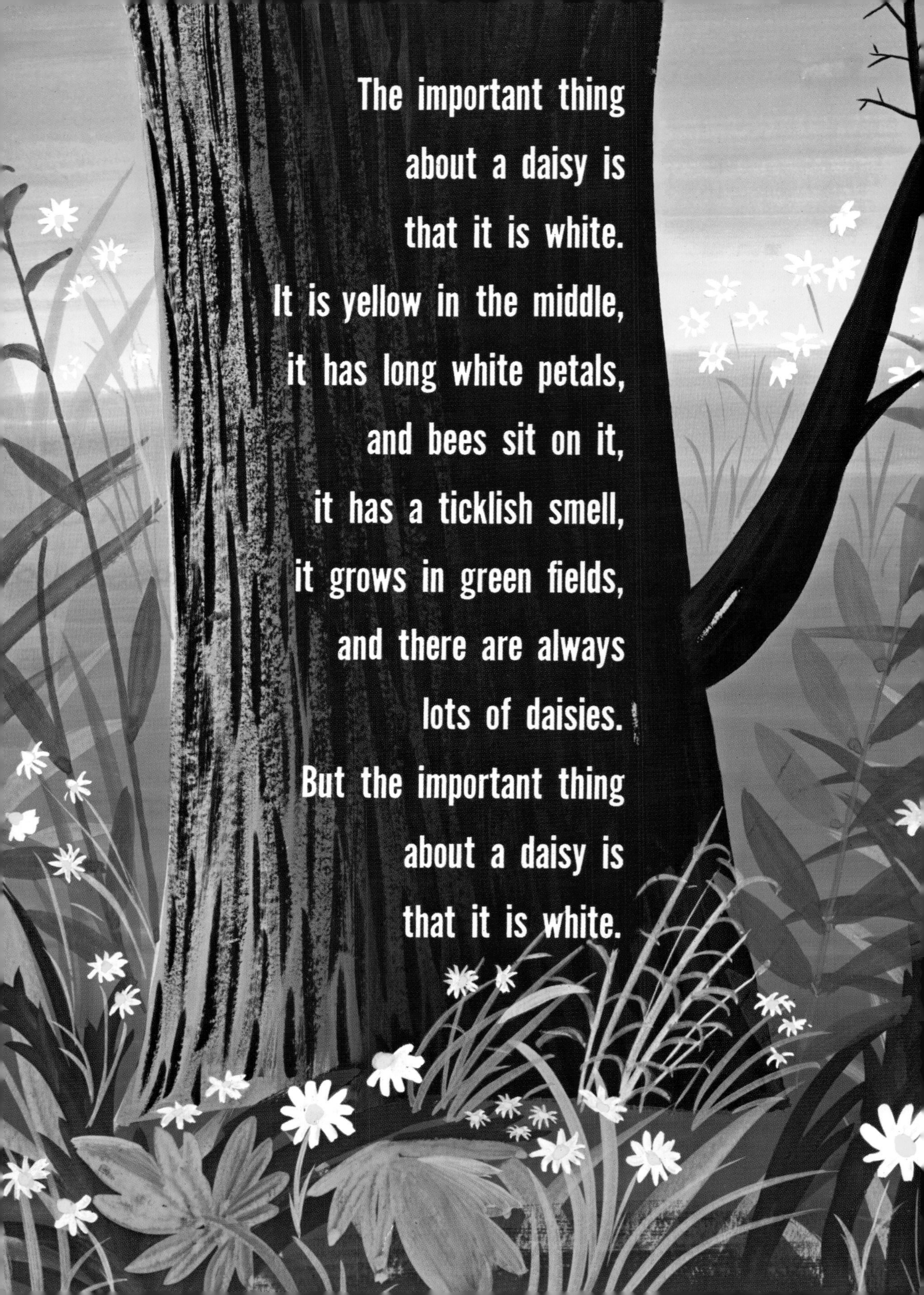

The important thing
about a daisy is
that it is white.
It is yellow in the middle,
it has long white petals,
and bees sit on it,
it has a ticklish smell,
it grows in green fields,
and there are always
lots of daisies.
But the important thing
about a daisy is
that it is white.

The important thing about rain is

that it is wet.

It falls out of the sky,

and it sounds like rain,

and makes things shiny,

and it does not taste like anything,

and is the color of air.

But the important thing about rain

is that it is wet.

The important thing
about grass is that it is green.
It grows, and is tender,
with a sweet grassy smell.
But the important thing about grass
is that it is green.

The important thing about snow is that it is white. It is cold, and light, it falls softly out of the sky, it is bright, and the shape of tiny stars, and crystals. It is always cold. And it melts.

But
the important thing
about the snow is
that it is white.

The important thing about an apple
is that it is round.
It is red.
You bite it,
and it is white inside,
and the juice splashes in your face,
and it tastes like an apple,
and it falls off a tree

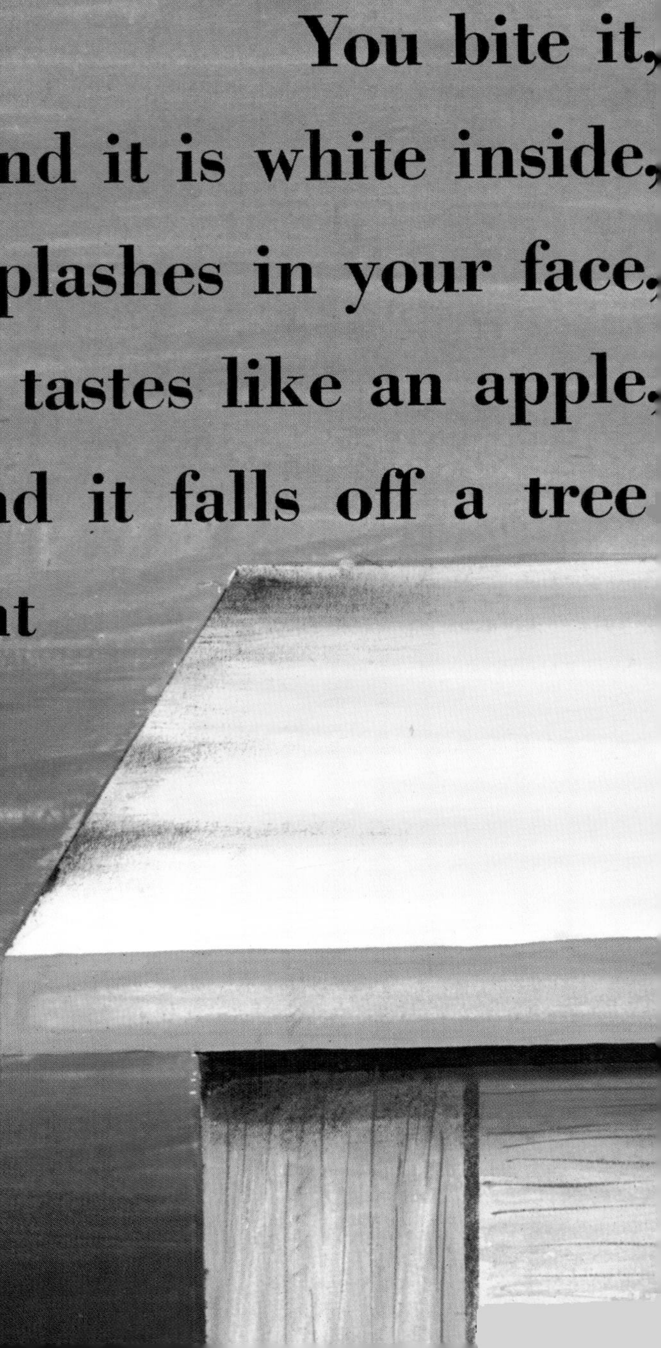

But the important
thing about
an apple is
that it is
round.

The important thing about the wind is that it blows. You can't see it, but you can feel it on your cheek, and see it bend trees, and blow hats away, and sail boats.
E
S
N
W

BUT
THE IMPORTANT THING
ABOUT THE WIND IS
THAT IT BLOWS.

The important thing
about the sky is that it is always
there. It is true that it is blue,
and high, and full of clouds,
and made of air.
But the important thing about
the sky is that it is always there.

The important thing about a shoe

is that you put your foot in it.

You walk in it,

and you take it off at night,

and it's warm when you take it off.

But the important thing about a shoe

is that you put your foot in it.

The important thing about you is

that you are you.

It is true that you were a baby,

and you grew,

and now you are a child,

and you will grow,

into a man,

or into a woman.

But the important thing about you

is that

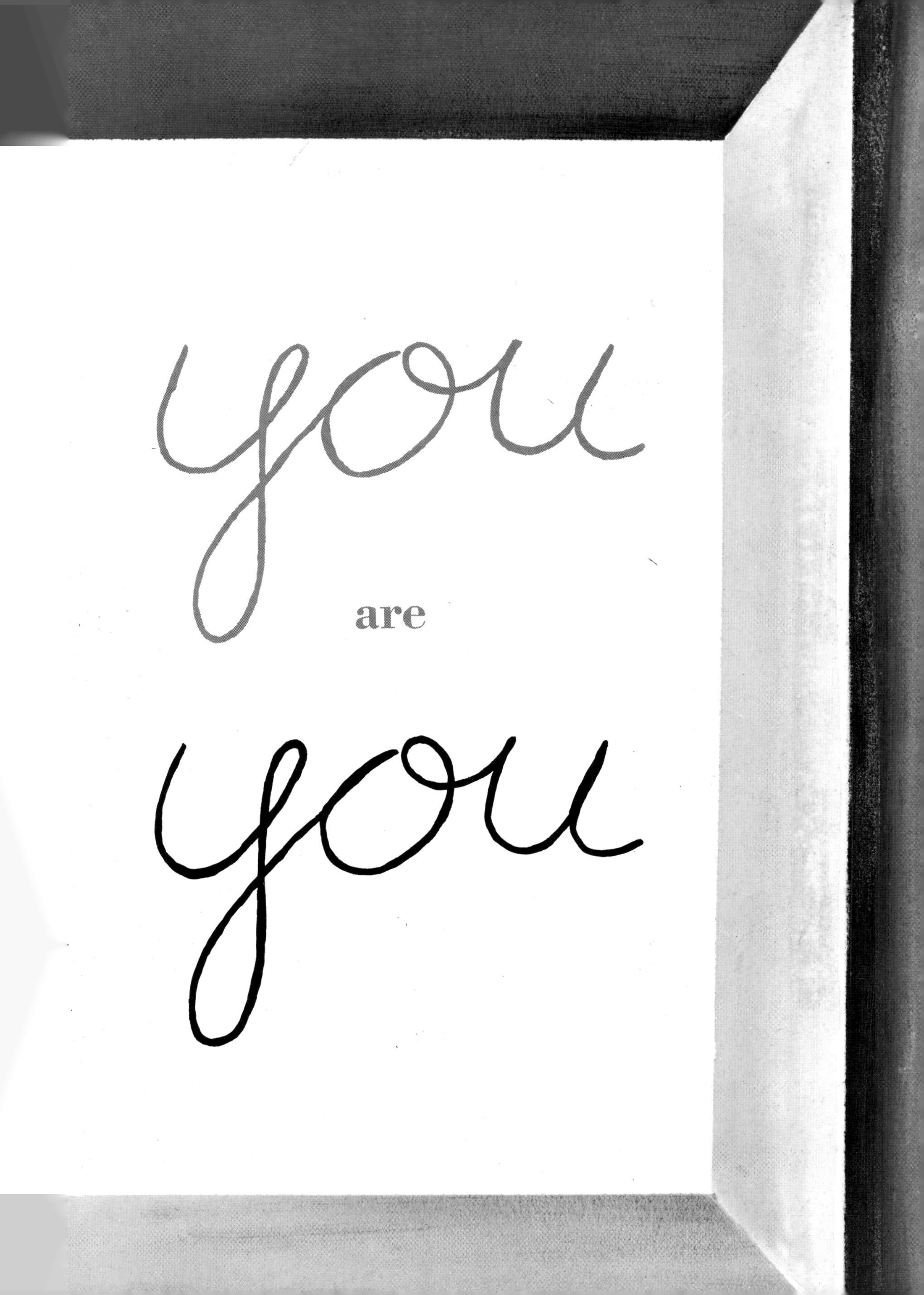

you

are

you